JF
Berenstain, Stan.
The Berenstain Bear Scouts
and the ripoff queen

The Berenstain Bear Scouts and the ripoff
JF Berenstain   49840
Berenstain, Stan,
    Goodland Public Library

DATE DUE

FEB 0 4 1999		
MAR 1 0 2000		
FEB 1 9 2001		
NOV 1 9 2001		
DEC 0 3 2001		
DEC 1 4 2001		
JAN 1 7 2002		
APR 2 8 2003		
MAR 0 6 2008		

GAYLORD   PRINTED IN U.S.A.

Look for more books in
The Berenstain Bear Scouts series:

*The Berenstain Bear Scouts
in Giant Bat Cave*

*The Berenstain Bear Scouts
and the Humongous Pumpkin*

*The Berenstain Bear Scouts
Meet Bigpaw*

*The Berenstain Bear Scouts
Save That Backscratcher*

*The Berenstain Bear Scouts
and the Terrible Talking Termite*

*The Berenstain Bear Scouts
and the Coughing Catfish*

*The Berenstain Bear Scouts
and the Sci-Fi Pizza*

*The Berenstain Bear Scouts
Ghost Versus Ghost*

*The Berenstain Bear Scouts
and the Sinister Smoke Ring*

*The Berenstain Bear Scouts
and the Magic Crystal Caper*

*The Berenstain Bear Scouts
and the Run-Amuck Robot*

*The Berenstain Bear Scouts
and the Ice Monster*

*The Berenstain Bear Scouts
and the Really Big Disaster*

*The Berenstain Bear Scouts
Scream Their Heads Off*

*The Berenstain Bear Scouts
and the Evil Eye*

THE Berenstain BEAR SCOUTS

and the
Ripoff Queen

by Stan & Jan Berenstain
Illustrated by Michael Berenstain

A
LITTLE APPLE
PAPERBACK

SCHOLASTIC INC.
New York Toronto London Auckland Sydney
Mexico City New Delhi Hong Kong

If you purchased this book without a cover, you should be aware that this book is stolen property. It was reported as "unsold and destroyed" to the publisher, and neither the author nor the publisher has received any payment for this "stripped book."

No part of this publication may be reproduced in whole or in part, or stored in a retrieval system, or transmitted in any form, or by any means, electronic, mechanical, photocopying, recording, or otherwise, without written permission of the publisher. For information regarding permission, write to Scholastic Inc., Attention: Permissions Department, 555 Broadway, New York, NY 10012.

ISBN 0-590-94493-2

Copyright © 1998 by Berenstain Enterprises, Inc.
All rights reserved. Published by Scholastic Inc.
LITTLE APPLE PAPERBACKS and associated logos
are trademarks of Scholastic Inc.

12 11 10 9 8 7 6 5 4 3 2   8 9/9 0 1 2 3/0

Printed in the U.S.A.   40

First Scholastic printing, December 1998

• Table of Contents •

1. Ralph's New Scheme   1

2. Mayor-for-a-day   10

3. A Telltale Clue   16

4. Abuse of Power   21

5. Where There's Ralph, There's Money   25

6. Split Down the Middle   31

7. The Lawyers Four   37

8. Public Relations Wars   45

9. Scouts to the Rescue   51

10. Bogged Down   60

11. Into the River   66

12. River Pirates!   71

13. Run Aground   78

14. Thanks for the Memories   92

THE Berenstain BEAR SCOUTS

and the
Ripoff Queen

• Chapter 1 •
Ralph's New Scheme

Ralph Ripoff was Beartown's resident
small-time crook and swindler. Beartown
folks had a saying about him: "Ralph's as
honest as the day is long . . . on the short-
est day of the year." So when Ralph
showed up at Mayor Honeypot's office
bright and early one summer morning, the
mayor knew right off that something
shady was in the works.

"Have a seat, Ralph," said the mayor,
motioning to a chair in front of his desk.
"What's on your mind?"

Ralph leaned forward and stared right

into Mayor Honeypot's eyes. "I'm going to say two words, Mr. Mayor," he said, "and I want your reaction. *Riverboat gambling*."

Mayor Honeypot's eyes lit up, and a smile came to his face. He had been known to do a little gambling from time to time. "My reaction is positive," he said. "Where can I get some of this action?"

"Nowhere this side of Big Bear City,"

said Ralph. "And that's exactly my point, Mr. Mayor. Beartown sorely needs a little excitement. Something to get the old blood flowing, not to mention the adrenaline. And what better way to do that than riverboat gambling?"

Mayor Honeypot's smile faded. "I know where you're going with this, Ralph," he said, "so I'll thop you right stare — er, I mean, stop you right there." He had a way of getting the fronts and backs of his words mixed up. "If you're thinking of turning that old stuck-in-the-mud house-boat of yours into a riverboat gambling operation, forget it. Gambling's illegal not just in Beartown itself but in the entire district, which includes Grizzly River. I would have thought you'd learned that by now, seeing as how often Chief Bruno has pent you sacking — I mean, sent you packing — with that phony shell game of yours."

GOODLAND PUBLIC LIBRARY
GOODLAND, KANSAS 6773⁵ ·

Ralph held up a hand. "Now, hold your horses, Mr. Mayor. Yesterday afternoon I went down to our public library and did some research on this very subject. It seems that the Beartown district line extends only to the *midline* of Grizzly River. I could keep the riverboat on the *other* side of the midline. The side that comes under the authority of the National Forestry Department."

"Hmm," said the mayor. "Are you allowed to run a gambling business on National Forestry Department land?"

"I don't know," said Ralph. "And that's why I came to you."

"But I don't know anything about the forestry department's regs and rululations — er, rules and regulations," said the mayor. "Why don't you just phone them and ask?"

"Have you ever heard the saying 'Let sleeping dogs lie'?" asked Ralph.

"Sure," said the mayor. "What's your point?"

"Suppose the forestry department has no rules against gambling in their territory," said Ralph. "If they find out someone is planning to set up a big operation like this, they might put in a new rule against it before I can get it under way."

"I see," said the mayor. "But I still don't see where I come in."

"Let's just call it 'legal aid,'" said Ralph. "You see, I'm hoping to score — er, *raise* — the money for this little venture from Lady Grizzly. But I know she'd never put money into such a thing unless she were certain it was all perfectly legal. The problem is, I can't afford to hire some hotshot lawyer to do the legal research."

"So you want me to spend fublic punds — er, public funds — to hire lawyers to check it out," said Mayor Honeypot.

Ralph nodded. Then he took a bulging envelope from the inside pocket of his jacket and handed it to the mayor. "This isn't nearly enough to pay the lawyers, but it's everything I won in a poker game last night," he said.

"You wouldn't be trying to bribe me, would you, Ralph?" said the mayor, with a wink.

"Perish the thought!" said Ralph, winking back. "Just think of it as advance payment for your appearance at the grand opening of the *River Queen*. You can cut the ribbon, make a long, boring speech, even use some of the advance to wager on the first spin of the roulette wheel, or the first hand dealt at the blackjack tables, or the first hundred pulls of a slot machine handle."

Suddenly the door swung open. With a gasp, Mayor Honeypot slipped the envelope into his jacket. "Well, well," he said brightly. "If it isn't Brother Bear and his little Bear Scout friends! Don't you cubs know the meaning of the word *knock*?"

Brother stood in the doorway, with the other scouts close behind. "I'm sorry, Mr. Mayor," he said. "I didn't think you'd come to work today. We're here to take over — I mean, *start work*."

"You're a few minutes early," said Mayor Honeypot. "Close the door and have a seat in the waiting room. I'll call for you shortly."

When the door had closed Ralph said, "What's this all about? *Take over?* Was there an election that I missed?"

"Oh, no," said the mayor. "Brother Bear just won Beartown's Mayor-for-a-day Contest by writing the prizewinning essay on 'Why I Want to Be Mayor-for-a-day.' The moment he found out he'd won, he appointed his fellow Bear Scouts assistant mayors. Cute, eh?"

"Very cute, indeed," said Ralph, with a sigh of relief. Then he frowned. "Does this mean my 'legal aid' is going to get held up? I'm meeting Lady Grizzly tomorrow morning. . . ."

"Hmm," said Mayor Honeypot. "I *was* planning to go fishing today. . . ." He patted the inside pocket of his jacket. "Tell you what I'll do, Ralph. I'll postpone my fishing trip and get right on this 'legal aid' thing." He leaned forward across his desk and lowered his voice. "But only if we forget this *advance payment* stuff."

"Huh?" said Ralph. "What do you mean?"

"I mean," answered the mayor, "only if we think of what you just gave me as a *down* payment. With the rest — say, ten times as much — to come one month after the *River Queen* opens for business. By then you'll be rolling in dough."

Ralph smiled nervously. "You drive a hard bargain, Mr. Mayor," he said. "But it's a deal."

"Good," said Mayor Honeypot. "Now send in those Bear Scouts, and I'll be on my way to the lawyers' office."

• Chapter 2 •

Mayor-for-a-day

Brother Bear snatched a cigar from
Mayor Honeypot's cigar box, popped it into
his mouth, and put his feet up on the
mayor's desk. He leaned back in the
mayor's swivel chair, hands clasped behind his head, grinning around the cigar.

"Hey!" snapped Sister Bear. "Take that
filthy thing out of your mouth!"

"Don't you mean, '*Please* take that
filthy thing out of your mouth, *Mr. Mayor,
sir*'?" said Brother. "Come on, Sis, I'm just
playing."

"Well, I'm not," said Sister. "Cigars give me the creeps."

"Okay, okay," said Brother, tossing the cigar into the wastepaper basket beside the desk.

"Don't you think it's time you told us why you barged in on Mayor Honeypot like that?" said Lizzy Bruin.

"Boy!" said Brother. "One minute as mayor and already I'm swamped with complaints! I couldn't talk about it in the waiting room, guys. The receptionist might have heard me."

"So talk about it now," said Cousin Fred.

"When I went to knock," said Brother, "I heard Ralph Ripoff's voice. So I listened for a moment. The first word I heard clearly was 'riverboat.' I tried to open the door a crack to hear better. But my hand slipped on the knob, and the door swung wide open."

"Ruining our chances of finding out what those two are up to," said Sister.

"Not completely," said Brother. "If the door hadn't opened all the way I wouldn't have seen the mayor slip a bulging envelope into his jacket."

"Aha!" said Fred. "Where there's a bulging envelope, there's money. Especially when Ralph is involved. Do you think he's cooked up a phony riverboat business scheme and got the mayor to invest in it?"

"No," said Brother. "I forgot to tell you: The second word I heard clearly was 'bribe.'"

"What's that mean?" asked Lizzy.

"*Bribe*," said Fred, who read the dictionary for fun. "*To give money to someone in a position of power or authority in return for a favor.*"

"So Ralph must have been bribing the mayor," said Lizzy. "Because the mayor has a lot of power."

"Yeah," said Sister. "And all Ralph's got is his broken-down houseboat, his obnoxious parrot, and the shirt on his back."

"Don't forget the tricks up his sleeve," cracked Brother.

"I don't get it," said Fred. "If Ralph wants to start a riverboat transportation business, why would he have to bribe Mayor Honeypot?"

"I don't know," said Brother. "But my first official act as mayor will be to find out. Now, my schedule is full for today. This morning I'm giving a TV interview, at lunch I have a hospital fund-raiser, and in the afternoon I'm giving a speech at the Beartown Press Club. So you three are going to have to do all the investigating, at least until tomorrow."

"Fine," said Fred. "But where do we start?"

The scouts thought for a while. Suddenly Sister said, "I've got it! Yesterday afternoon I saw Ralph come out of the public library."

"Hmm," said Brother. "Ralph at the public library. Sounds pretty fishy, considering that Ralph never reads anything except *Swindler's Digest* and he has a subscription to that. I want you guys to go

down there and talk to the librarian.
Maybe you can get her to tell you what
books Ralph checked out. Then report
back to me."

"Right, Mr. Mayor!" said Sister, standing at attention and saluting smartly.

The cubs giggled as they filed out of
their boss's office.

• Chapter 3 •
A Telltale Clue

As it turned out, Beartown's three assistant-mayors-for-a-day had no trouble getting Ms. Goodbear the librarian to answer their question about which books Ralph had checked out the day before. The only problem was the answer: none.

"Maybe he stole a couple," suggested Sister.

"Oh, no," said Ms. Goodbear. "Our staff kept a very close eye on Mr. Ripoff while he was here. No one could remember him ever coming in before, but we all knew his reputation."

"We'd better let you in on something," Fred told Ms. Goodbear. "We're not just here as Bear Scouts. We're here in our official capacity as assistants to Mayor-for-a-day Brother Bear, and we're investigating a possible crime. So anything you can tell us about what Ralph did here yesterday could be very important."

"Oh, my goodness," said Ms. Goodbear. "Well, let me think. Oh, yes, I remember now. Mr. Ripoff asked me to show him the legal section and help him find a book on Beartown laws. I did just that, and he spent about half an hour looking through a particular law book. It may not have been reshelved yet. Let's go see."

The scouts followed Ms. Goodbear to the legal section, where they checked the return shelves. On one of them rested a thick leather-bound volume entitled *Laws of Grizzly River County. Volume I:*

Beartown, Bearville, and Bruinville Districts.

"Yes," said Ms. Goodbear. "This is the one Ralph looked through. Now, if you'll excuse me, I must get back to the front desk. Good luck."

The scouts carried the heavy volume to a nearby table and began to read. They

had barely gotten through five pages of dense legal language when Sister shook her head. "This is a wild-goose chase," she said. "There must be four hundred pages on Beartown in this book. How are we going to figure out what Ralph was looking for?"

But just then Fred turned a page and cried, "Aha!"

"Shhh," said Lizzy. "This is a library, remember?"

"*Aha,*" Fred whispered. "Here's a page corner that's been turned down. I'll bet Ralph did that so he could find this page again after going through the rest of the Beartown stuff. Let's see if there are any other corners turned down."

There weren't. Fred turned back to the one he'd found. "Hmm," he said. "It's about the gambling laws. It says that at one time gambling was outlawed only within the city limits of Beartown, but now it's illegal in the entire district. Then it says to see Appendix IV for a map showing the city and district boundaries."

"Gambling?" said Sister. "That sure sounds like Ralph."

"Hmm," said Fred. "*Gambling. River-boat . . .*" Suddenly his eyes lit up. "Of course! *Riverboat gambling!* Ralph wants to turn his houseboat into a riverboat gambling business!"

"Yeah!" said Sister. "And when he found out that gambling is outlawed in the entire district, he decided to bribe Mayor Honeypot to look the other way!"

"Just wait till we tell the mayor-for-a-day about this!" said Lizzy. "He can break this case wide open to the Press Club this afternoon!"

• Chapter 4 •

Abuse of Power

Scouts Sister, Lizzy, and Fred had lunch at the Burger Bear, then headed for Town Hall. They found Brother in the mayor's office, practicing his speech for the Press Club.

"What's the title of your speech, Mr. Mayor?" asked Sister.

"'Programs for Cubs in Beartown,'" replied Brother.

"Well, I've got a new title for you," said Sister. "'*Corruption at Town Hall'!*"

But when she had finished telling

Brother about what they'd found out at the library, he looked worried.

"What's wrong?" asked Fred. "We thought you'd be really excited."

"It's a good first step," said Brother. "But we can't go accusing Ralph and Mayor Honeypot of something just because of a turned-down page corner in a library book. Besides, I can't go straight to the press with this. I have to tell Chief

Bruno first and let him do a proper police investigation."

"Then pick up the phone and call him," insisted Lizzy.

"Now, hold on," said Brother. "We may have to wait on that."

"*Wait?*" said Sister. "*Now* is the time to do it — while you're mayor-for-a-day! You can *order* Chief Bruno to investigate!"

Brother shook his head. "Investigating Ralph is one thing," he said. "But I'm not sure we want to put Chief Bruno in the position of having to investigate his own boss. He might think we were abusing our power-for-a-day."

The other scouts could see Brother's point. They thought for a while. Finally Fred said, "I have an idea. Let's try to get more evidence on Ralph and the mayor, then tell our folks about it and get *them* to put pressure on Chief Bruno to investigate. That would carry more weight than a bunch of cubs making accusations."

The scouts agreed on the wisdom of Fred's suggestion. And Brother came up with a plan for getting more evidence. "Let's tail Ralph tomorrow," he said. "We'll hide in the tall grass near his houseboat and wait for him to come out."

"What if he sees us following him?" asked Sister.

"Simple," said Brother. "We just tell him we're on a scouting hike. Now, let's go to the Press Club. I could use some moral support for my speech."

This time all three of the assistant-mayors-for-a-day stood at attention and saluted. "Right, Mr. Mayor!" they chorused.

• Chapter 5 •

Where There's Ralph, There's Money

"Too bad there isn't a Corruption Fighters Merit Badge Award," said Sister as the Bear Scouts huddled in the tall grass behind Ralph's houseboat the next morning.

"True," said Brother. "But don't forget, Sis: Bear Scouts are supposed to be good citizens, not just trophy collectors. Hey, here he comes!"

Ralph emerged from the houseboat and strolled down the gangplank to the path that ran along the riverbank. He had a spring in his step. He twirled his cane and whistled a tune as he ambled down the path and disappeared into the woods.

"He sure looks happy," said Sister. "Where do you suppose he's going?"

"Somewhere where there's *money*," said Brother. "Come on, let's go."

The scouts followed Ralph at a safe distance all the way into town. At first they thought he was headed for Town Hall, but he bypassed Town Hall and went into the Beartown Museum of Fine Art.

"The art museum?" said Lizzy as the scouts hurried up the front steps. "There's no money in here. Just a lot of paintings and sculptures."

"Don't be so sure," said Brother. "Where there's Ralph, there's money."

When the scouts entered the museum lobby, they saw that Brother was right. For there, coming out of the gift shop, was none other than Lady Grizzly, the richest woman in Bear Country, arm in arm with none other than Ralph Ripoff.

"They're going into the Gallery of Portraits," said Brother. "Come on."

The scouts crossed to the gallery entrance and peered in. Lady Grizzly and Ralph were already on the opposite side of

the gallery, gazing up at a huge portrait of a naked lady bear reclining on a couch. They were too far away for the cubs to hear them. But the portrait was right next to the gallery exit, so the scouts hurried through the next gallery and found their way to the exit of the Gallery of Portraits. Brother peeked around the corner at Lady Grizzly and Ralph.

"I don't hear anything," whispered Sister.

"They're not talking," Brother whispered back. "Ralph's standing there blushing."

Then they heard Lady Grizzly's voice: "But this is great art, Ralph. Why in the world wouldn't you like it?"

"It's — er, uh — showing a little too much fur for my taste," said Ralph.

"Oh, Ralph," said Lady Grizzly. "I didn't know you were such a prude. Now, what did you want to talk with me about?"

"Lady Grizzly," said Ralph, "I know how long you've been living in the shadow of your super-successful husband, Squire Grizzly. And I know how much you've fretted over the way he looks down on you as nothing but a rich wife with a bunch of expensive hobbies."

"How did you know?" said Lady Grizzly.

"Beartown folks have been gossiping about it for years, my dear," said Ralph. "But you needn't fret any longer. Because with my help you're going to become a successful businessbear in your own right. Why don't we have a seat on that bench over there while I explain my proposal?"

The voices moved off toward the center of the gallery.

"Darn!" said Sister. "Now we won't hear what Ralph is up to!"

"We don't need to hear any more," said Fred. "It's obvious. Ralph needs a lot of money to start up his illegal gambling business, and he's trying to get it from Lady Grizzly."

"Do you think she'll go for it?" asked Lizzy.

"It sounds like she just might," said Fred.

"I agree," said Brother. "I say it's time to let our folks in on this. Before Lady Grizzly gets in any deeper. We should tell Scout Leader Jane, too." He looked at his watch. "In fact, we have a scout meeting with her in fifteen minutes. Let's go."

The scouts made their way back to the main entrance and hurried to Scout Leader Jane's house.

• Chapter 6 •

Split Down the Middle

Scout Leader Jane was horrified when she heard of Ralph's plan. She told the scouts she would go see Chief Bruno first thing the next morning.

Later, at the dinner table in their tree house, Brother and Sister told Mama and Papa — and Gran and Gramps, who were visiting — all about their suspicions. They had expected that all four of the grown-ups would be up in arms over Ralph's plan. What actually happened, however, was quite different.

True, Mama and Gran immediately

spoke out against Ralph's plan. "If Ralph starts riverboat gambling on Grizzly River," said Mama, "it'll be a dark day for Beartown."

"You can say that again," added Gran. "I know quite a few folks in this town who've had their problems with gambling in the past."

But Papa and Gramps didn't join in. Instead, they just sat there with dreamy looks in their eyes.

"Papa," said Mama, "didn't you hear what Brother and Sister said?"

"Huh?" said Papa. "Brother and Sister? Oh, yeah, sure. Riverboat gambling, eh?" He rubbed his hands together. "Roulette, dice, blackjack, poker . . ."

"Don't forget keno and slot machines," added Gramps with a smile. "Remember that system for winning at blackjack we talked about years ago, son? Well, now's our chance to give it a try!"

"Gramps!" said Gran. "I can't believe my ears!"

"Nothin' wrong with gambling," said Gramps. "Heck, everything in life's a gamble."

"But in *life* the odds aren't usually a million to one against you like they are in all these casinos," said Gran. "Besides, if I remember correctly, you've had your problems with gambling even when the odds were a lot better than a million to one. When I first met you, you were always blowin' your paychecks on poker with the guys. That's why *I* always wound up paying for our dates!"

Gramps looked sheepish and sulky at the same time. "That was a long time ago," he mumbled. "I was young and foolish then."

"And now it's different," said Gran. "Now you're *old* and foolish!"

"Hold on, Gran," said Papa. "Gramps is

right. We're responsible bears. We know how to control our gambling." He jerked his thumb at the window behind him. "The bear you should be worried about is our neighbor."

"Farmer Ben?" said Mama.

"Didn't you know, dear?" said Papa. "Right after Ben inherited the farm from his father, he almost lost it in a poker game."

"Oh, my goodness!" said Mama. "That does it. Gran, tomorrow morning you and I are going down to the police station to have a little talk with Chief Bruno. Gambling is illegal in Beartown District, and that includes Grizzly River. The chief can put a stop to this before it starts."

Just then the phone rang. Mama answered it. "Mrs. Bruin!" she said. "Oh, yes, that's a wonderful idea. Gran and I were just talking about doing that. Scout Leader Jane suggested it? I'll phone Mrs.

Ben and get her to come, too. We'll meet you and Jane in front of the police station bright and early." She looked up. Papa was waving at her. "Wait a second, Papa wants to talk to Biff."

Phone in hand, Papa waited until Mama and Gran were busy doing the dishes in the kitchen. "Hey there, Biff, how

are you? Listen, Gramps and I were just thinkin' about getting a little poker game together for tomorrow night. We haven't played in a while, and suddenly we feel the urge. You can? Great. Can you round up a couple other guys . . . ?"

By now Brother and Sister had heard enough. They went upstairs to their room.

"Boy!" said Brother, plopping down on his bed. "It looks like the men and the women are headed in opposite directions."

"Yeah," said Sister. "And the men might as well be headed *over a cliff*!"

• Chapter 7 •

The Lawyers Four

When Mama, Gran, Mrs. Bruin, Mrs. Ben, and Scout Leader Jane met with Chief Bruin the next morning, it didn't take them long to convince him that Ralph's riverboat gambling plan had to be stopped.

"And we'd better move fast," said the chief. "With all the money Lady Grizzly has, Ralph could have this thing up and running in no time."

Chief Bruno didn't know the half of it. When he and the ladies arrived in his squad car at Ralph's houseboat, what they saw stunned them. There were Ralph and Lady Grizzly arm in arm, gazing up at a ramshackle houseboat covered with work-bears hammering, sawing, and measuring. A second story was being added to *Ralph's Place*.

"Well, well," said Ralph when he noticed the visitors. "Citizens of Beartown, welcome! It looks as if word of our exciting business venture has leaked out to the public."

"*Slithered* out, you mean," muttered Gran.

"Lady Grizzly," said Chief Bruno, "how in the world did Ralph get you to invest in an illegal business?"

"Illegal?" said Lady Grizzly. "Oh, no. It's nothing of the kind. Ralph checked that out thoroughly."

"But gambling is illegal in the entire district of Beartown," said the chief. "And that includes Grizzly River."

"Yes," said Ralph, "But only *part* of Grizzly River. . . ."

Just then a car drove up, and four bears in business suits got out. Each carried a briefcase.

"Good to see you, fellas," said Ralph. "Do you have a copy of that memo you faxed me a couple of days ago?"

One of the bears produced a sheet of paper from his briefcase and handed it to Ralph, who handed it to Chief Bruno. The chief read it aloud. This is what it said:

From: Quarrel, Quarrel, Quarrel, and Quibble
Attorneys-at-Law
To: Mr. Ralph Ripoff
Re: Gambling on Grizzly River

The Beartown District antigambling laws extend only to the midline of Grizzly River: The riverbank to which your houseboat is moored is under the authority of the National Forestry Department. We have made a thorough check of all Forestry Department rules and regulations and have found none that prohibits gambling.

Chief Bruno shook his head. "I don't believe it," he mumbled.

"But it's true," said the first Quarrel.

"Absolutely," said the second Quarrel.

"Positively," said the third Quarrel.

"Without a doubt," added Quibble.

"You see?" said Ralph. "It's all perfectly legal."

"This is a disaster!" cried Gran. "We're just gonna have to find some other way to stop it!"

"I wouldn't advise that," said the first Quarrel.

"You could get in trouble —" said the second Quarrel.

"— if you interfere with a legal business," said the third Quarrel.

"*Big* trouble," added Quibble.

"Say," said Ralph, turning to the lawyers, "have you fellas ever sung any barbershop quartets? I might be able to use you in the floor show."

"You're going to have a floor show?" said Mama.

"Floor show, fine dining, dancing, the works!" said Ralph. "This isn't going to be any ordinary casino. Oh, no. This'll be the *best*. Classy, respectable, a paragon of business virtue! You are no longer looking at Ralph Ripoff, small-time crook and swindler. You are looking at Ralph Ripoff, president of River Queen Incorporated!"

"And *I'm* Chairbear of the Board!" added Lady Grizzly with a giggle.

"Respectable?" gasped Mama. "You call riverboat gambling respectable? It may be *legal*, but that doesn't make it *respectable*. You're the same Ralph Ripoff you always were, taking Beartown folks for a bunch of suckers."

"I bet all the slot machines will be rigged, too," said Scout Leader Jane.

"No, no," said Lady Grizzly. "Ralph

assured me that everything will be on the up-and-up."

"Yeah," muttered Gran. "And a lot of Beartown folks'll be *down-and-out*."

"Come on, ladies," said Chief Bruno. "There's nothing we can do. At least not here and not now."

They marched to the squad car. Once inside, Gran leaned out of the window and called back, "I think you should name that darn boat after yourself, Ralph!"

"You mean *Ralph's River Queen*?" said Ralph. "Hmm. Catchy."

"No!" called Gran. "I mean the *Ripoff Queen!*"

As the squad car drove off, Ralph turned to Lady Grizzly with a sheepish grin. "Bad idea," he said. "Folks might get the wrong impression."

• Chapter 8 •

Public Relations Wars

Work on the *River Queen* was completed in record time. At the grand opening, Mayor Honeypot cut the ribbon and made a long-winded speech about the fun and excitement that riverboat gambling would bring to Beartown. Then the gambling started.

Like any first-class casino, the *River Queen* was open for business twenty-four hours a day, seven days a week. "Nonstop gambling," Ralph called it in his newspaper ads and TV commercials. But if the gambling never stopped, the *River Queen*

did. It ran from the north end of Beartown
to the south end, and every time it
reached the south end it stopped briefly to
take on customers and fresh crew and
staff. They boarded from a motorboat that
ran from a dock Ralph had built. The motorboat first took the crew and staff out to

the *River Queen*, then returned for the customers. Ralph had designed everything to work smoothly. And it did.

But there was one problem that Ralph hadn't counted on. At first only the "serious" gamblers visited the *River Queen*. That's because Chief Bruno managed to

scare away others by mounting a public relations campaign against the *River Queen*. He went on TV and radio and gave newspaper and magazine interviews, claiming over and over that the gambling machines on the *River Queen* — the slot machines, the keno machines, and the poker machines — were rigged so that it was almost impossible to win.

But then Ralph counterattacked. *He* went on TV and radio and gave newspaper and magazine interviews, claiming over and over that his gambling machines were *not* rigged and that Chief Bruno didn't have a shred of evidence to prove that they were. He even challenged the chief to come to the *River Queen* himself and check out the machines.

Ralph's counterattack worked, at least partly. Quite a few bears were persuaded to try the *River Queen*. But still not enough to suit Ralph.

Way too many to suit Chief Bruno, on the other hand. So he called a meeting at the police station with the top members of AARG, the Alliance Against Riverboat Gambling. The group had been formed by Mama Bear, Grizzly Gran, Scout Leader Jane, and their friends. It had been joined by most of Beartown's wives.

"I know Ralph's bluffing," the chief told the ladies. "His machines *are* rigged, I'm sure of it. He just doesn't think I'll take him up on his challenge to check them out."

"Then why not call his bluff?" asked Mama.

"I can't," said the chief. "What do *I* know about machines?"

The AARG members thought for a while in silence. Suddenly Mrs. Bruin thrust a finger into the air. "I've got it!" she said. "Who's the only bear in Bear Country who knows all there is to know about machines?"

Mama's eyes lit up. "Of course! Professor Actual Factual!"

"And he's right here in Beartown, at the Bearsonian Institution!" added Gran.

Chief Bruno phoned Actual Factual's office at the Bearsonian right away. The professor agreed to help and said he was free that very afternoon. The chief then phoned the media. Now he and AARG had Ralph right where they wanted him. . . .

• Chapter 9 •

Scouts to the Rescue

When Chief Bruno and Professor Actual
Factual showed up at the *River Queen*
with a BNN (Bear News Network) camera
crew in tow, Ralph had no choice but to allow the professor to examine the gambling
machines. He could see that a *BNN-live*
special report was already underway, and
he wasn't about to make a wrong move
while his own nervous smile was being
telecast all over Bear Country.

But the surprise visit didn't turn out
the way Chief Bruno and AARG had
hoped. When Actual Factual checked the

machines, he found each of them in perfect working order. None of them had been tampered with.

The *BNN-live* report from the *River Queen* was a disaster for Beartown's antigambling forces. AARG immediately stopped its campaign. And Chief Bruno actually hid in his office for a few days. (Some folks had already given him a new nickname: Bonehead Bruno.) Meanwhile, customers poured into the *River Queen*. Ralph was so busy keeping an eye on the casino that he scarcely had time to eat or sleep.

About a week after the *BNN-live* telecast, the Bear Scouts met for after-dinner shakes at the Burger Bear. Soon they got to talking about the *River Queen*.

"I heard that Too-Tall and his gang sneaked in a couple of nights ago," said Fred. "They said it was still packed at four o'clock in the morning."

Sister shook her head sadly. "I guess Ralph and Lady Grizzly win," she said.

"Maybe Ralph wins," said Brother. "But I'm not so sure about Lady Grizzly."

"What do you mean?" asked Lizzy.

"I overheard Mama talking to Gran on the phone last night," said Brother. "It seems that Squire Grizzly has turned into a gambling fanatic. He's been losing thousands of dollars at the *River Queen* every night for a week now. I'll bet Lady Grizzly is having second thoughts about the whole thing."

"And did you hear about Farmer Ben?" asked Fred. "My mom says he just mortgaged his farm to pay off his gambling debts at the *River Queen*. And some of his crops are starting to rot in the fields because he's at the *Queen* all day when he should be working."

"Same goes for Papa," said Sister. "He and Gramps have been on the *River*

Queen all day and night three days in a row now. They've had all their meals on the boat."

Brother nodded. "The orders for new furniture are piling up in Papa's workshop. And it isn't just Papa and Gramps and Squire Grizzly and Farmer Ben. It seems like *most* of the men in town have been bitten by the gambling bug."

"We've got to do something!" said Sister. "We've got to shut down the *River Queen!*"

"But how?" asked Lizzy.

The scouts thought for a while. Suddenly Fred looked up with a twinkle in his eye. "I've got an idea," he said. "What would happen if the *River Queen* accidentally crossed the midline of Grizzly River and Chief Bruno saw it?"

"That's easy," said Brother. "The chief would arrest Ralph and all the gamblers and shut down the *River Queen.*"

"Exactly," said Fred. "So all we have to do is get the *Queen* to cross the midline."

"Oh, is *that* all?" sneered Sister. "And how in the world would we do that?"

"Here's how," said Fred. "When the *Queen* gets to the south end of town it stops to take on fresh staff and new customers. That's when *we* slip into the river and rig the rudder so that when the *Queen* starts up again it steers over the midline. And we arrange it so that Chief Bruno is waiting on the other side of the river to arrest Ralph and confiscate all his gambling equipment. Of course, we can't tell the chief beforehand what we're planning to do."

"Why not?" asked Sister.

"Because tampering with the *River Queen* can't be legal," said Fred. "The chief might keep us from doing it."

"Uh-oh," said Brother. "You're right." He

looked at each of the others in turn. "Well, what do you guys think? Is it still worth a try?"

"I don't know," said Lizzy. "As Bear Scouts, we're sworn to uphold the law."

"No, we're not," said Sister. "It doesn't say that in the Bear Scout Oath."

"It may not be in the letter of the oath," said Brother, "but it's sort of in the spirit of the oath."

"And the oath says a Bear Scout 'plays the game fair and clean,'" said Lizzy.

"This isn't a game," said Sister. "This is real life. Ralph tries to make riverboat gambling look like a game. But it's really legalized stealing. That's why Gran calls the *River Queen* the *'Ripoff Queen.'* The oath also says a Bear Scout 'always respects the rights of others.' Don't we have to respect the right of Beartown folks not to be legally robbed?"

"I agree," said Fred. "If we don't do this, a lot of families in this town will go broke."

"Including ours!" said Sister.

Now Brother and Lizzy were convinced. But Brother wondered whether it was even possible to rig the *Queen's* rudder. It would probably take more than a few minutes to do, and the rudder was completely underwater. Wouldn't they drown?

"I've already thought of that," said Fred. "Actual and Ferdy Factual use scuba-diving gear whenever they study algae in Great Grizzly Lake. We could go to the Bearsonian tomorrow morning and borrow it. They may have extra gear. And I'll bet Actual Factual will know the easiest way to rig the rudder, too."

"I've got to hand it to you, Fred," said Brother. "This is the greatest idea in gambling history."

"Don't you mean in *anti*gambling history?" said Fred.

The scouts laughed. Then Brother said it was time to do the Bear Scout cry. So they crossed their drinking straws over the table and shouted, "One for all, and all for one!"

• Chapter 10 •
Bogged Down

The next morning, while the Bear Scouts were already on their way to the south end of town from the Bearsonian, something strange was happening farther north on Grizzly River. As the *River Queen* eased its way along the swampy stretch where *Ralph's Place* had once been moored, a rowboat pulled up alongside it. Three rough-looking characters in overalls and floppy hats boarded the riverboat and made their way toward Ralph's office. One of them stopped for a moment to glance through a porthole-shaped window into the casino, but the gamblers inside were too caught up in their "games" to notice.

When the bears reached Ralph's office they didn't bother to knock. They barged right in.

"Well, I'll be!" said Ralph, looking up in surprise from behind his desk and dropping the money he had been counting. "If it isn't my good friends the Bogg Brothers. Finally decided to visit my fabulous floating casino, eh? Hope you brought plenty of cash with you, boys."

There was a grin on Ralph's mouth but fear in his eyes. The Bogg Brothers, who lived in an old shack deep in Forbidden Bog, were some of the roughest customers in all of Bear Country. Over the years they had been involved in all kinds of crime, from drug running to trapping endangered species for their pelts.

"Didn't bring no cash," muttered Billy Bogg, the oldest.

"What a shame," said Ralph nervously. "Of course, I'd be happy to give you fellas some casino credit —"

"Hush up!" growled Billy. "We didn't come to gamble. We came to fix your gamblin' machines."

"Fix them?" said Ralph. "But there's nothing wrong with them. They're in perfect working order, and the odds are set to Bear Country casino standards."

"That's what's wrong with 'em," said Billy Bogg. "Only a fool sets the odds to casino standards. We're gonna fix 'em so the odds are three times worse for the customers. That way we'll triple our take."

"*Our* take?" said Ralph, tugging at his collar.

"That's right," said Billy. "From now on you, me, and Bobby and Bert here are in business together. You're gonna keep runnin' the casino, but *we're* gonna get most of the money. You can have ten percent. Just think of me as your new boss. How's that sound?"

"Do I have a choice?" said Ralph in a high, squeaky voice.

"Sure," said Billy. "You can either go along with it or get bound and gagged and thrown overboard right now. Well, what's it gonna be?"

Ralph gulped and took a deep breath. "Since you put it that way," he said, "I'll go along with it."

"Good," said Billy. "I *thought* you'd see it our way." Bobby and Bert snickered. "Now, when we get to the south end of town, you're gonna show all the customers into the bar and tell 'em the casino is closed for repairs for a few minutes. Got that?"

"Got it — er, boss," said Ralph, raising his hand in a sheepish salute. "I'll have the bartender serve them each a free Jackpot — that's what we call our famous secret-recipe cocktail. But first I need to speak with my captain about the delay so he can alert the crew."

"Go ahead," said Billy. "And make it snappy."

Ralph hurried to the wheelhouse, where Captain Kodiak was steering the boat. He told the captain about the delay.

"What's going on?" asked the captain.

"No time to explain," said Ralph, lowering his voice. "I want you to write the following message on a slip of paper and give it to one of the crew and tell him to get it to Lady Grizzly: *Bogg takeover, machines rigged.* Got that?"

The captain nodded.

"Tell him to use one of the lifeboats and be quiet about it," said Ralph. "*Immediately.*"

Ralph went into the casino and herded the gamblers into the bar. There was a lot of grumbling — especially from Papa Bear, Grizzly Gramps, Farmer Ben, and Squire Grizzly — even after they were served their free Jackpots.

• Chapter 11 •
Into the River

It was a good thing the Bear Scouts had gone to Actual Factual for equipment and advice. Rigging the rudder of a big river-boat like the *River Queen* is no easy thing, and the scouts would never have figured out all by themselves how to do it. The professor had given them a rope and some large eye hooks. They would screw one of the hooks into the rudder and the other into the underwater overhang of the boat's stern. Then they would tie the rope to the hooks in such a way that the ship would steer slightly to the right. They had to be

careful not to let the boat steer too sharply
to the right, because then it would just go
in circles and might never cross the midline.

Now they were crouching in the cattails
along the riverbank near the dock at the
south end of town. Soon the *River Queen*
came into view upriver.

"Here she comes," said Brother. "Let's
get ready."

The scouts wriggled into their scuba-diving gear. All except for Lizzy. She had volunteered to run to the police station and tell Chief Bruno that the *River Queen* had crossed the midline. If they timed it perfectly, the chief would arrive just as the *Queen* reached the opposite bank of the river.

Brother fastened a sack holding the eye hooks to a loop on his suit. Cousin Fred tied the rope around his waist.

Now the *River Queen* was almost directly in front of them. It slowly turned around and stopped. The scouts could clearly see Captain Kodiak leave the wheelhouse and walk off toward the bow of the boat.

"There he goes," said Fred. "That's our cue."

"Boy, will *he* be surprised when he tries that steering wheel again," said Brother.

Now the scouts could hear the motorboat carrying fresh staff to the *Queen*. They peeked over the cattails and saw a cluster of riverboat customers at the dock, waiting for the motorboat to return.

"It's time," announced Brother. "Off you go, Lizzy."

Lizzy crawled out of the cattails and ran north along the riverbank to where she could cross to town on Grizzwin Bridge.

"Don't forget," said Brother. "When the *Queen* starts moving again, we follow it across the river. I want to be there to see Ralph's face when Officer Marguerite claps the handcuffs on him."

"But won't we get arrested, too?" said Sister.

"For tampering with the *Queen*?" said Brother. "Probably. But a scout is 'as honest as the day is long,' according to the Bear Scout Oath. If we're going to do something illegal, we should accept the consequences. The main thing is that we know what we're doing is right."

The scouts put on their face masks and checked their oxygen tanks. Then they slipped silently into the cold water of Grizzly River.

From the riverbank the *Queen* had looked so close. But now the scouts felt as if they had to swim forever to get to it. After a while its stern loomed ahead through the murky water. They swam directly to the rudder and set to work.

The scouts worked as fast as they could. But every second they were thinking: Will we be able to finish the job before the *Queen*'s engines start up again?

• Chapter 12 •
River Pirates!

As the scouts worked underwater, something very strange was happening back at
the dock. The moment the motorboat
reached it, a group of bears dressed in
pirate outfits leaped from the nearby
bushes and rushed it. "Stay away from
that boat!" cried the leader, brandishing a
cutlass. "It's ours!"

The would-be gamblers gasped but then
backed away, laughing, as the pirates piled
into the boat and headed off toward the
River Queen. "That's great!" said one gam-

bler to another. "Ralph has hired actors to play a band of pirates taking over the *River Queen*! What'll he think of next?"

Aboard the *River Queen*, Ralph was sitting with his elbows on his desk and his head in his hands when Captain Kodiak came bursting into his office.

"Boss!" cried the captain. "We've got a band of river pirates in the casino!"

Ralph looked up wearily. "Those are the Bogg Brothers, you idiot!" he growled.

"No!" said the captain. "The Bogg Brothers are down in the bilge, changing the electrical wiring to the casino. These are real river pirates! With pistols and cutlasses!"

With Captain Kodiak on his heels, Ralph ran to the casino as fast as his spats could carry him. He got there just in time to see two of the pirates dropping a slot machine overboard.

"Stop, thief!" cried Ralph.

"Thief?" said one of the pirates. "We're not *stealin'* it! We're *trashin'* it!"

Ralph turned to Captain Kodiak. "I know that voice!" he said. "It's Grizzly Gran! These aren't river pirates! They're AARG members!"

Just then two of the other pirates dropped a keno machine overboard, and a third pair heaved a poker machine into the river.

"Quick!" said Ralph to the captain. "Get the Bogg Brothers! They'll put a stop to this!"

But Captain Kodiak was one step ahead of his boss. He had already disappeared below. Moments later he reappeared, huffing and puffing. "Someone's padlocked them in the bilge!" he gasped.

"That was me," said a pirate who sounded a lot like Scout Leader Jane.

"When we didn't see them right away, we figured they were down there."

"But how did you know they were even on the boat?" said Ralph.

"Lady Grizzly told us," said Jane.

"Take this roulette wheel," said a pirate with Mama Bear's voice, handing it to Jane. "I'll get the other one." Together they threw the wheels over the side.

"Hey, Ralph," said Gran, "maybe you should go into *underwater* gambling!"

Meanwhile, blackjack tables and more machines were going into the drink. At last only one machine was left. Ralph stepped in front of his pride and joy, the jumbo-size Big Jackpot slot machine. "Keep away!" he cried. "You're not taking my baby!"

Gran aimed her plastic pirate pistol at him. "Outta the way, Ralph!" she snarled. "Everything goes!"

But Ralph's attention was already elsewhere. "Why are we moving?" he yelled at Captain Kodiak.

"I ordered the crew to start the engines as soon as the motorboat pulled away the second time," said the captain. "And I never had time to cancel the order!"

"Hey, we're not just moving!" cried Ralph. "We're going off course! Go grab that steering wheel, Captain! *Quick!*"

Captain Kodiak hurried off to the wheelhouse. In a moment he was back, huffing and puffing again. "It's stuck!" he gasped.

As the pirates began dragging Big Jackpot toward the railing, Ralph dashed to the wheelhouse. He grabbed the wheel and tried to turn it to the left. It wouldn't budge. He pulled and tugged and pulled again. Still nothing. "Oh, no!" he cried. "This is a disaster!"

Ralph looked wildly around. The *Queen* had already crossed the river's midline and was headed straight for the opposite bank. Ralph ran crazily from the wheelhouse. "Look out!" he screamed at the top of his lungs. "We're gonna crash!"

• Chapter 13 •
Run Aground

Ralph threw himself facedown on the
deck and covered his head with his hands.
But the pirates paid no attention to his
warning. They were too busy struggling
with Big Jackpot. They hauled it up to the
top of the railing, where it teetered, about
to go over.

All the dragging and hauling must have upset Big Jackpot's innards. Because all of a sudden a bell like a fire alarm went off. The pirates were looking right at the place on Big Jackpot's belly where the symbols showed, and they saw that three honeypots had come up. An instant later, the machine began spitting silver dollars. Out they came in a steady stream, clanking and clattering on the deck.

Before long the pirates were ankle-deep in silver dollars. At last they got Big Jackpot leaning toward the river. Over it went, still burping up coins here and there as it hit the water with a tremendous splash and sank like a rock.

Fortunately, the crew had shut down the *River Queen*'s engines in midriver, so the big boat wasn't going fast enough to crash into the bank. Instead, it eased into the bottom mud and came gently to rest without so much as a creak.

At the same time, Chief Bruno's squad car arrived, and the chief, Officer Marguerite, and Lizzy Bruin got out. Mama Bear lowered the gangplank so they could climb aboard, as the gamblers finally filed out of the bar, some of them still clutching their Jackpot cocktails.

Ralph leaped to his feet when he saw Chief Bruno. "I can explain everything, Chief!" he said. "It was an accident! We never meant to cross the midline! And it was the Bogg Brothers who rigged my machines! I did nothing wrong! Don't arrest me!"

Chief Bruno looked around. "Arrest you?" he said. "Why would I do that? I don't see any slot machines or roulette wheels or blackjack tables. I don't even see any gambling going on. Anyone have a pair of dice?"

The gamblers eagerly held out their empty hands, palms up.

"All I see," continued the chief, "is a huge pile of silver dollars. Do you have a license to carry coins as cargo, Ralph?" Ralph shook his head. "Then I'm afraid I'm going to have to confiscate all this money."

The "pirates" broke into applause. "You tell him, Chief!" yelled Gran.

"They're the ones who trashed my machines!" cried Ralph. "Arrest them!"

"Consider yourself lucky they trashed your machines, Ralph," said Chief Bruno. "If they hadn't, I would have arrested *you*. Now, the Bogg Brothers are another story. I have a month-old warrant for their arrest right here in my pocket. They've been making moonshine in Forbidden Bog and selling it in all the river towns within a hundred miles of here. Where did they go after they tampered with the machines?"

Scout Leader Jane told the chief that she had locked them in the bilge. The chief sent Officer Marguerite down with the key. Soon the surly brothers emerged with their hands in the air. Marguerite was behind them, her pistol at the ready.

"Well, we finally caught up with you goons," said Chief Bruno. "Cuff 'em, Marguerite!"

Officer Marguerite handcuffed the Bogg Brothers and led them down the gangplank to the squad car. Just then a chauffeured limousine drove up, and out stepped Lady Grizzly. She boarded the *River Queen* and went straight to her husband. She stood glaring at him, hands on hips.

Squire Grizzly tipped his hat and gave a sheepish grin. "Hello, dear," he said. "Looks like my gambling is done for the day."

"Looks like your gambling is done *forever*," she corrected him. "Now, get in the car!"

As the squire slunk off to the limousine, Lady Grizzly turned to the other gamblers. "You ought to be ashamed of yourselves," she said, "gambling at eleven o'clock in the morning when you should be at your jobs. Put a pair of dice or a slot machine handle in your hands, and all your common sense goes right out the porthole!"

Lady Grizzly smiled at the "river pirates." "Lovely outfits," she said. "Beartown Theatrical Supply?" They nodded.

Then she turned to Ralph. "When I got your note," she explained, "I picked up the phone to call Chief Bruno. But then I realized he had no authority on the other side of Grizzly River. So I called AARG instead. It looks as if they've done a very thorough job on the *Queen*."

"Indeed they have, Lady Grizzly," said Ralph. "But that needn't put an end to the *Queen*'s travels. If you, my dear, would put up some more money, we could replace all the machines and tables in no time —"

"Dream on, Ralph!" snapped Lady Grizzly. "After what this so-called business venture did to my husband and to the husbands of these other good women, I wouldn't invest another *dime* in it! However, I *will* put up the money to have the *River Queen* converted back into *Ralph's Place. Provided* you take it back to its proper spot in the swamp and leave it right there for the rest of its ramshackle life. And yours. That's my offer. Take it or leave it."

Ralph hung his head and mumbled, "I'll take it."

All of a sudden three strange underwater creatures emerged from the river and mounted the gangplank on floppy, flippered feet. They weren't really strange underwater creatures, of course. They were the Bear Scouts, minus Lizzy.

The three scouts went straight to Officer Marguerite and held out their wrists. "Cuff us, Marguerite," said Brother. "We're

the ones who tampered with the *River Queen*'s rudder."

"Hold on, Marguerite," said Chief Bruno. "You cubs did all your tampering on the other side of the river, didn't you?" They nodded. "Well, I have no authority over there. And I doubt very much that the National Forestry Department is going to bother itself with a minor local incident like this one."

"Then we're free to go?" said Brother.

"Absolutely," said the chief. "And even if I *could* charge you with a crime, there isn't a jury this side of Big Bear City that would convict you. Not after all the havoc the *River Queen* caused for Beartown folks. Personally, I think you cubs deserve medals."

"A wonderful idea!" boomed a familiar voice coming up the gangplank. It was Mayor Honeypot. "Let me be the first to congratulate you cubs!" He shook the

A WONDERFUL IDEA!

hand of each scout in turn, then those of
the AARG members. "You, too, ladies!"

The mayor was an experienced hand-
shaker, and he made a good show of it.
"You *all* deserve medals," he proclaimed,
"for ridding our town of the scourge of
riverboat gambling!" It was only then that
he noticed he was standing in silver dollars. "What's all this?"

"Ralph's Big Jackpot machine went crazy," said Chief Bruno. "I'm confiscating all of it for the city."

"Right quite," said the mayor. "Er — I mean, quite right. And *I* shall recommend to the town council that this money be placed in a special fund to aid the families of the *Ripoff Queen*'s many victims."

A cheer went up not just from the scouts and the AARG members but from

the gamblers, too. And no one cheered
louder than Papa Bear, Grizzly Gramps,
and Farmer Ben.

"And don't forget me at election time!"
added Mayor Honeypot when the cheering
died down.

The scouts thought back to the meeting
in the mayor's office they had barged in on
earlier that month. They just looked at
one another and winked.

• Chapter 14 •

Thanks for the Memories

It was amazing how quickly things returned to normal in Beartown. The Bear Scouts went back to their normal scouting activities. Mayor Honeypot went back to making long, boring speeches and lots of election promises. Squire and Lady Grizzly went back to their businesses and charity work. Farmer Ben went back to his fields. Papa Bear went back to his carpentry, and Grizzly Gramps went back to his model-ship building. Even Ralph Ripoff returned to normal, going back to his shell game and other small-time swin-

dles. All as if the *River Queen* had been little more than a dream.

Actually, that wasn't quite true in
Ralph's case. Fond memories of the *River
Queen* lingered in his mind for quite a
while. Memories of tumbling dice and
spinning roulette wheels, and of flickering
honeypots on Big Jackpot.

One of the things that kept Ralph's
memories alive was his pet parrot,
Squawk. Since the *River Queen*'s casino
had been directly above *Ralph's Place*,
Squawk had overheard a great deal of
what went on during those long days and
nights of gambling on the river. From time
to time, while Ralph lounged on the sofa,
reading the latest issue of *Swindler's Digest*, Squawk would suddenly cry out,
"Double or nothing! Double or nothing!" or
"We have a winner! We have a winner!"
That would make Ralph look up from his
magazine and think back to all those won-

drous days and nights on his beloved *River Queen*.

But it wasn't only the sounds of gambling that Squawk had picked up. Every once in a while he would pipe up with, "Look out! We're gonna crash! Look out! We're gonna crash!"

At that, Ralph would yell, "Shut up, birdbrain! Don't remind me!" Then he would bury his face in *Swindler's Digest*, reflect on ways to improve his shell game and his five-card-monte swindle, and do his very best to banish from his mind all thoughts of riverboat gambling.

• About the Authors •

Stan and Jan Berenstain have been writing and illustrating books about bears for more than thirty years. Their very first book about the Bear Scout characters was published in 1967. Through the years the Bear Scouts have done their best to defend the weak, catch the crooked, joust against the unjust, and rally against rottenness of all kinds. In fact, the scouts have done such a great job of living up to the Bear Scout Oath, the authors say, that "they deserve a series of their own."

Stan and Jan Berenstain live in Bucks County, Pennsylvania. They have two sons, Michael and Leo, and four grand-children. Michael is an artist, and Leo is a writer. Michael did the pictures in this book.

THE Berenstain BEAR® SCOUTS
by Stan & Jan Berenstain

Join Scouts Brother, Sister, Fred, and Lizzy as they defend the weak, catch the crooked, joust against the unjust, and rally against rottenness of all kinds!

❏ BBF60384-1	The Berenstain Bear Scouts and the Coughing Catfish	$2.99
❏ BBF60380-9	The Berenstain Bear Scouts and the Humongous Pumpkin	$2.99
❏ BBF60385-X	The Berenstain Bear Scouts and the Sci-Fi Pizza	$2.99
❏ BBF94473-8	The Berenstain Bear Scouts and the Sinister Smoke Ring	$3.50
❏ BBF60383-3	The Berenstain Bear Scouts and the Terrible Talking Termite	$2.99
❏ BBF60386-8	The Berenstain Bear Scouts Ghost Versus Ghost	$2.99
❏ BBF60379-5	The Berenstain Bear Scouts in Giant Bat Cave	$2.99
❏ BBF60381-7	The Berenstain Bear Scouts Meet Bigpaw	$2.99
❏ BBF60382-5	The Berenstain Bear Scouts Save That Backscratcher	$2.99
❏ BBF94475-4	The Berenstain Bear Scouts and the Magic Crystal Caper	$3.50
❏ BBF94477-0	The Berenstain Bear Scouts and the Run-Amuck Robot	$3.50
❏ BBF94479-7	The Berenstain Bear Scouts and the Ice Monster	$3.50
❏ BBF94481-9	The Berenstain Bear Scouts and the Really Big Disaster	$3.50

© 1997 Berenstain Enterprises, Inc.

Available wherever you buy books or use this order form.

Send orders to:
Scholastic Inc., P.O. Box 7502, Jefferson City, MO 65102-7502

Please send me the books I have checked above. I am enclosing $_____ (please add $2.00 to cover shipping and handling). Send check or money order — no cash or C.O.D.s please.

Name _____ Birthdate ___/___/___
M   D   Y

Address_____

City _____ State _____ Zip_____

Please allow four to six weeks for delivery. Offer good in U.S.A. only. Sorry, mail orders are not available to residents of Canada. Prices subject to change.

BBSE897

LITTLE 🍎 APPLE®

Here are some of our favorite Little Apples.

Once you take a bite out of a Little Apple book—you'll want to read more!

Books for Kids with BIG Appetites!

- ❑ NA45899-X **Amber Brown Is Not a Crayon**
  Paula Danziger **$2.99**
- ❑ NA42833-0 **Catwings** Ursula K. LeGuin **$3.50**
- ❑ NA42832-2 **Catwings Return** Ursula K. LeGuin **$3.50**
- ❑ NA41821-1 **Class Clown** Johanna Hurwitz **$3.50**
- ❑ NA42400-9 **Five True Horse Stories** Margaret Davidson **$3.50**
- ❑ NA42401-7 **Five True Dog Stories** Margaret Davidson **$3.50**
- ❑ NA43868-9 **The Haunting of Grade Three**
  Grace Maccarone **$3.50**
- ❑ NA40966-2 **Rent a Third Grader** B.B. Hiller **$3.50**
- ❑ NA41944-7 **The Return of the Third Grade Ghost Hunters**
  Grace Maccarone **$2.99**
- ❑ NA47463-4 **Second Grade Friends** Miriam Cohen **$3.50**
- ❑ NA45729-2 **Striped Ice Cream** Joan M. Lexau **$3.50**

Available wherever you buy books...or use the coupon below.

- -

SCHOLASTIC INC., P.O. Box 7502, 2931 East McCarty Street, Jefferson City, MO 65102

Please send me the books I have checked above. I am enclosing $ _____ (please add $2.00 to cover shipping and handling). Send check or money order—no cash or C.O.D.s please.

Name_____

Address_____

City_____**State/Zip**_____

Please allow four to six weeks for delivery. Offer good in the U.S.A. only. Sorry, mail orders are not available to residents of Canada. Prices subject to change.   LAP198